Bing

ATCHOO!

HarperCollins *Children's Books*

This Bing book belongs to:

The *Bing* television series is created by Acamar Films and Brown Bag Films
and adapted from the original books by Ted Dewan.

ATCHOO! is based on the original story written by Helen Farrall, Lucy Murphy, Mikael Shields and Ted Dewan.
It was adapted from the original story by Lauren Holowaty for HarperCollins *Children's Books*.

HarperCollins *Children's Books* is a division of HarperCollins*Publishers* Ltd
1 London Bridge Street, London SE1 9GF

www.harpercollins.co.uk

HarperCollins*Publishers*
Macken House, 39/40 Mayor Street Upper, Dublin 1, D01 C9W8

1 3 5 7 9 10 8 6 4 2

ISBN: 978-0-00-861949-7

Printed and bound in the UK

This book is produced from independently certified FSC™ paper
to ensure responsible forest management.

For more information visit: www.harpercollins.co.uk/green

Round the corner, not far away,
Bing has **exciting plans** today!

BUMP!
SNIFF!

BUMP!
SNIFF!

BUMP!
SNIFF!

"Is it time to go to Sula's house?" Bing asks Flop, sniffing loudly as he bounces down the stairs.

"Yup," replies Flop. "Let's go!"

"Amma said she would make me a special carroty bagel!" says Bing.

AAAAA-TCHOO!

"Eichi!" says Flop. "That nose of yours sounds sniffly, Bing. Are you okay?"

"Yup. Let's go to Sula's," says Bing. Then he sneezes again . . .

ATCHOO!

As Flop opens the front door,
a **great whoosh** of cold air blows in.

"*Ooof!* It's all wintry cold out there," says Flop,
shutting the door. "You'll need a coat, Bing."

ATCHOO!

Flop pulls out a tissue
and wipes Bing's nose.

As Flop helps Bing put on his coat,
he notices that Bing feels very hot.

"I'm not sure you **are** okay, Bing,"
says Flop. "You're all snottery."

"Let's go another day. You might give your germs
to Sula, and then she'll catch your cold," says Flop.

"Ohhhh," says Bing. "I *really* want
to see Sula and eat a carroty bagel!"

"I'm sorry, Bing," says Flop.

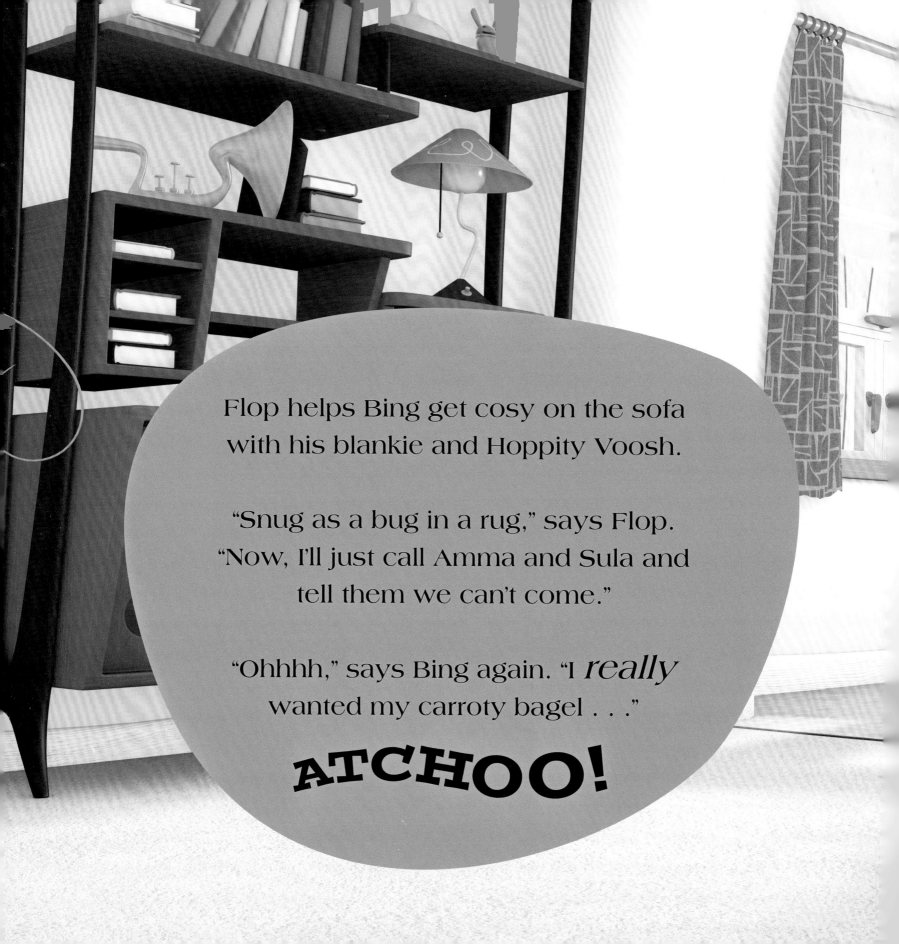

Flop helps Bing get cosy on the sofa with his blankie and Hoppity Voosh.

"Snug as a bug in a rug," says Flop. "Now, I'll just call Amma and Sula and tell them we can't come."

"Ohhhh," says Bing again. "I *really* wanted my carroty bagel . . ."

ATCHOO!

"Amma and Sula say they'll see you soon," says Flop.

"But I *really* . . . **sniff** . . . wanted to go to Sula's today," sighs Bing. **Atchoo!**

"Eichi!" says Flop, showing Bing how to catch his sneeze in a tissue. "How about you read your Hoppity Voosh book and I'll make you some hot honey and lemon? It'll make you feel better."

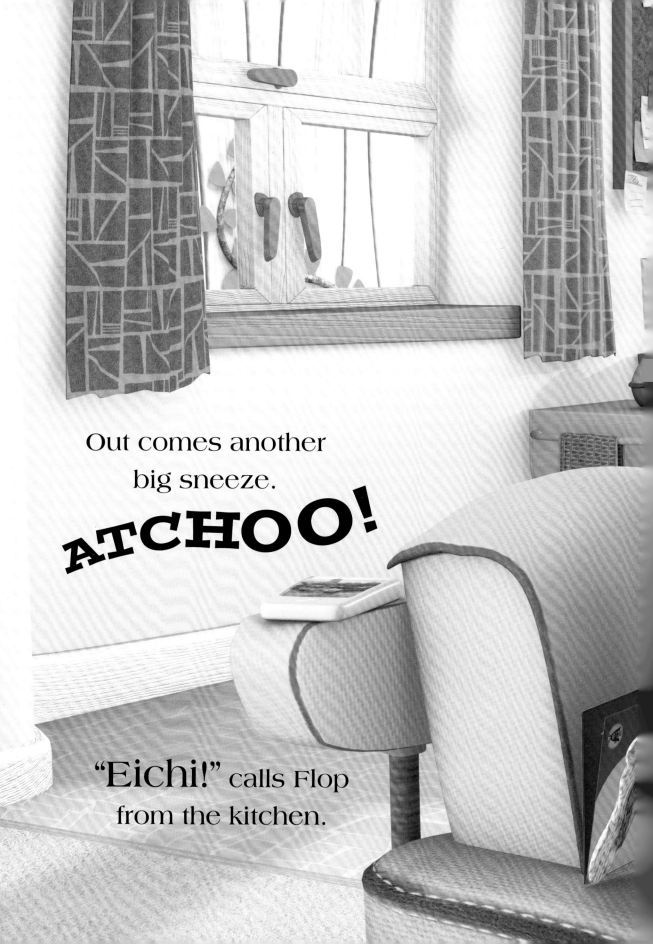

But Bing doesn't want to read his Hoppity Voosh book. He feels disappointed that he isn't at Sula's, and he hides under his blankie.

Out comes another big sneeze.

ATCHOO!

"Eichi!" calls Flop from the kitchen.

Just then, Bing
hears a noise . . .

Tap!
Tap!
Tap!

Bing peeks out from
under his blankie and
looks around, but
he can't see where
the tapping noise
is coming from.

Flop comes back with honey and lemon in Bing's favourite mug.

Bing sniffles and hears the same strange sound again.

Tap! Tap! Tap!

"What's that?" asks Bing. "I keep hearing that noise, Flop."

"Mmmm," says Flop. He's not sure what the sound is either.

"Bi-ing!" calls Sula, popping her head up at the window. "It's mee-ee!"

"Sula!" cheers Bing, waving.
"It's Sula, Flop!"

"Yes," says Flop, going over to open the window.

Sula and Amma have come to see how Bing is.

"Hello!" calls Amma. "Is there a germy bunny in there?"

"Yes, meee!" calls Bing. "I'm all *germish!*"

"Special delivery to help chase those germs away," says Amma. She hands a box to Flop for Bing.

Flop takes Amma's special
delivery over to Bing.

"It's to make you feel
better, Bing!" Sula calls
from the window.

Atchoo! sneezes Bing.

"Eichi!" say Flop and Amma together.

Bing opens
the box.
"Ahhh!
My carroty
bagel!"

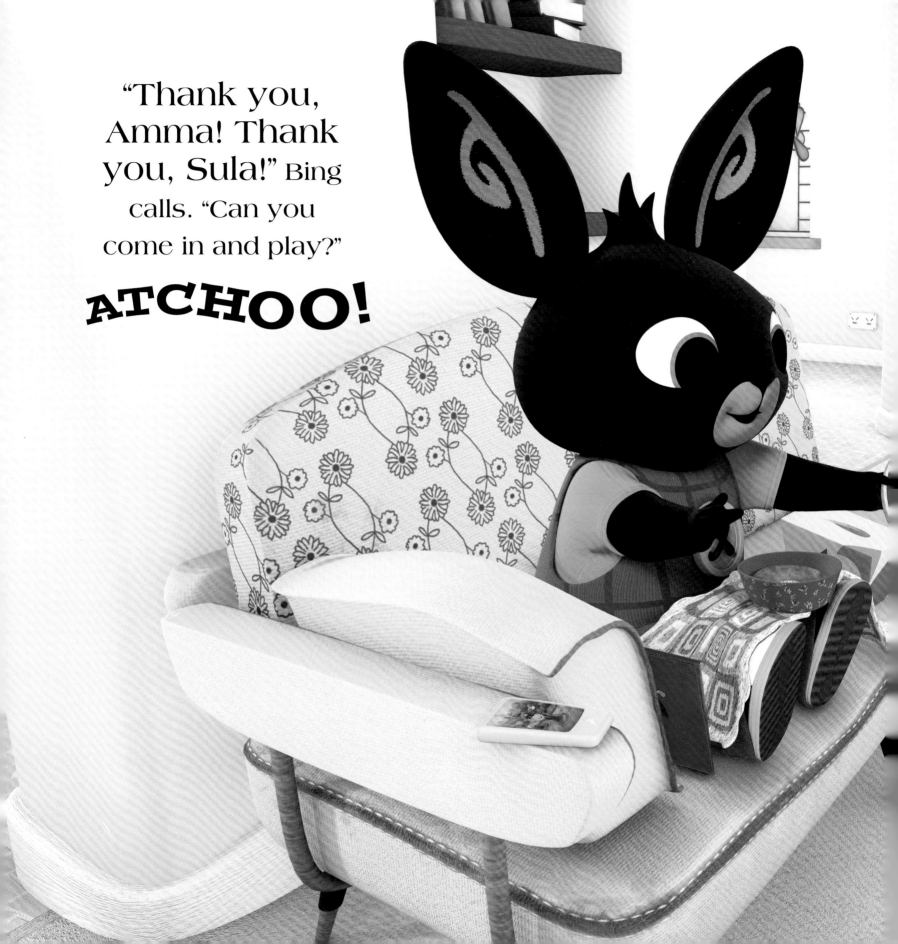

"Thank you, Amma! Thank you, Sula!" Bing calls. "Can you come in and play?"

ATCHOO!

"No, thank you, Bing,"
says Amma. "We don't
want your snotty-bobbles."

Bing and Sula both giggle.
"Snotty-bobbles!"

"Come and play with us
another day," says Amma.

*"Snotty-bobbles go
away, so Bing can
play another day!"*
sings Sula. "Bye, Bing!"

"Bye!" says Bing. "See you
when I'm all better."

Bing sits on the sofa with his carroty bagel. "Mmmm! Sula gave me my bagel, but I *didn't* give her my germs, Flop."

"Good for you, Bing Bunny!" says Flop.

Sneezes . . . they're a Bing thing!